"I was born in London in 1946 and grew up in a sweet shop in Essex. For several years I worked as a graphic designer, but in 1980 I decided to concentrate on writing and illustrating books for children.

My wife, Annette, and I have two grown-up children, Ben and Amanda, and we have put down roots in Suffolk.

I haven't recently counted how many books there are with my name on the cover but Percy the Park Keeper accounts for a good many of them. I'm reliably informed that they have sold more than three million copies. Hooray!

I didn't realise this when I invented Percy, but I can now see that he's very like my mum's dad, my grandpa. I even have a picture of him giving a ride to my brother and me in his old home-made wooden wheelbarrow!"

NICK BUTTERWORTH

PERCY'S FRIEND
THE HEDGEHOG

NICK BUTTERWORTH

HarperCollins *Children's Books*

Thanks Graham Daldry. You're a wizard.

Thanks Atholl McDonald. You're a hero!

First published in Great Britain by HarperCollins Publishers Ltd in 2001
ISBN-13: 978 0 00 778247 5
ISBN-10: 0 00 772247 0

Text and illustrations copyright © Nick Butterworth 2001
The author asserts the moral right to be identified as the author of the work.

Visit our website at: www.harpercollinschildrensbooks.co.uk

Printed and bound in Thailand by Imago

MY FRIEND THE HEDGEHOG

There are two things you get to know very quickly about the hedgehog. The first thing is that he is a lovely little chap. And the second thing is that he is a worrier.

He worries about all sorts of things. Loud noises. Being left out. And perhaps most of all, he worries about his prickles. He thinks they might put people off him. That's why he is always careful to say 'sorry' if he jabs someone accidentally.

His friend the badger keeps an eye on him and he gets on well with the mole.

He has a secret wish to fly like a bird. And he just loves balloons... but that's another story!

Not far from my hut there is an apple tree. In the autumn, when the apples are ripe, they sometimes drop to the ground before I can pick them.

One day, as I was having my lunch break, the hedgehog came to see me.

"I've brought you an apple," he said. "Could you take it off my head please?"

THE HEDGEHOG REALLY LIKES ...

Parties. But paper hats are not much good for a prickly head!

Flying. He may not be able to fly, but he loves to watch others who can.

THE HEDGEHOG DOESN'T LIKE ...

Having an itchy back. He can never
find anyone to scratch it for him!

Being left out. But there is usually
a way for him to join in.

One day, when I was out on one of my favourite walks, I came across the hedgehog right on the edge of the park.

He looked a little bit upset to me. He told me that somebody had got cross with him when he had bumped into them and accidentally prickled them.

He had decided to go exploring. He said he might be away exploring for quite a long time. I suggested that it might be better to go exploring after a sandwich at my hut.

He said he'd like that. He only had pine cones tied up in his explorer's bundle.

I've got lots of pictures in my photo album.

A windy autumn day. Not the hedgehog's favourite kind of weather!

I'm not sure if the hedgehog thought these were relations or if ne just likes conkers!

Here are some I took of my good friend, the hedgehog.

The hedgehog is very good at drawing pictures. He showed the fox how to do colouring without going over the edge. The fox said he liked going over the edge.

At first, I thought this was a cactus. Then I realised someone had got stuck in a flower pot!

Have you ever made a snow animal? I once made a snow hedgehog. My little friend was very excited to see a hedgehog that was nearly as big as me.

He asked how much he would have to
eat to grow up to be as big as my snow
hedgehog.

"Would it be as much as the fox eats
when we have a picnic?" he said. I told
him that I liked him the size he was.

A HEDGEHOG'S TALE

I'm in trouble with one of the ducks,
   I'm afraid she backed into my spines.
If you really must know where I jabbed her,
   It was just over there by those pines.

She wasn't too pleased and she said so.
   She said I should watch where I went.
I don't suppose it matters to her
   that three of my spines are all bent.

I sometimes wish I was different.
   I get so fed up with these prickles.
I wish I had lovely soft feathers,
   or a long furry tale that just tickles.

But my friend Percy always says,
   "I like your spines just as they are,
All pointed and spiky,
   do you know, little hedgehog,
     I think you're really. . . A STAR!"

FAVOURITE PLACES

When I asked the hedgehog to tell me some of his favourite places he just said, "Up in the air."

I wasn't sure what he meant and he couldn't stop to explain because he was late for an important meeting with the mole and Tootie.

I can only think that 'up in the air' is where he would most like to be. I know he'd love to be able to fly like a bird. And he has wonderful dreams where he has flying races with a couple of seagull friends.

One of his favourite places would be anywhere there is a swing. I don't think I know anyone who likes a swing more than the hedgehog. It must feel a bit like flying.

He needs a bit of help to get on, but then, if you see what I mean, he's off! The higher the better, he says. I think that's brave for a worrier...

Of course, the hedgehog loves his home in the tree house. He lives at the bottom of the tree, but often he'll go visiting higher up. You might even catch him up there swinging in his hammock!

Here he is, my friend the hedgehog,
relaxing with a lollipop. I wonder
where he got it. I also wonder who left
a paintbrush halfway up an oak tree!